VIKING
ADVENTURES

THE WORLD
TO THE WEST

Written and Illustrated by Andy Elkerton

W
FRANKLIN WATTS
LONDON • SYDNEY

Franklin Watts
First published in Great Britain in 2017 by
The Watts Publishing Group

Text and Illustrations © Andy Elkerton 2017

Series Editor: Melanie Palmer
Series Designers: Peter Scoulding
and Cathryn Gilbert

ISBN 978 1 4451 5838 9 (hbk)
ISBN 978 1 4451 5839 6 (pbk)

Printed in China

Franklin Watts
An imprint of
Hachette Children's Group
Part of The Watts Publishing Group
Carmelite House
50 Victoria Embankment
London EC4Y 0DZ

An Hachette UK Company
www.hachette.co.uk

www.franklinwatts.co.uk

Chapter One

Harald Forkbeard watched a flock of birds fly squawking overhead. He scratched his hairy chin and then pointed a finger at the horizon.

"We'll explore over there," he said to the Viking heroes, "to see the part of the world we've never been to before. We'll leave first thing tomorrow."

I'll bring trinkets, for trading.

Chapter Two

Next morning they boarded their sturdy
boat and set sail. When their home was
far out of sight, Erik heard a strange sound
coming from behind Agnar's fish barrels.
He went to have a closer look.

"Oolaf!" gasped Forkbeard. "What are you doing here?" he spluttered.

"Sorry Dad," mumbled Oolaf. "I left Mum a note, telling her exactly where I am."

Forkbeard groaned at the thought of the telling off he'd get when they got back home.

"Well now you're here you might as well do something useful," he sighed.

"Swab the deck!" he ordered.

After a few hours of scrubbing and mopping, Forkbeard decided Oolaf had suffered enough and called him to the helm. He showed Oolaf how to plot a course by the smell of the air ...

or the colour of the sea ...

or wherever the sun was.

On cloudy days he'd use his special *Sun Stone* to find where it was hiding, and at night, while the others sang songs and told stories, he showed Oolaf how to sail by the moon and stars.

One day, the sky went as grey as an axe
head. Forkbeard knew what that meant.
"Hold tight!" he shouted. "Here
comes a STORM!"

Great waves battered the boat. Oars snapped and sails tore as the boat began to groan and splinter.

Through the rain they spied dark shapes amongst the waves. "Sea Serpents!" cried Oolaf. There was a terrible CRUNCH! Then everything went black.

The five Vikings awoke on a strange beach
of pink rocks. A band of rather cross-looking
Natives surrounded them.

"Follow us," one of them ordered, holding
a long, sharp spear.

The Vikings gathered their things and followed. The Native village wasn't like anything they'd seen before. Everyone lived in little tents, and there were colourful totems of marvellous beasts. "We should make those back home," Oolaf whispered to his dad.

The Village Chief, Tuk, listened with
amazement as Forkbeard told him about
Viking houses, and about their voyage.
Ogbad gave him a handful of trinkets and
Agnar gave him a taste of pickled fish ...

"We will help you build your boat," Tuk spluttered, after his eyes stopped watering.

"But the Tribe on the Plains who could make a sail from animal skins, and the Tribe near The Great Lake who could weave some rope will never help, because we are enemies. They are an unfriendly bunch!"

Suddenly an idea popped into Oolaf's head. He quietly took Ogbad's trinket bag and a pouch of Agnar's fish, then tip-toed away from the tent and out of the village.

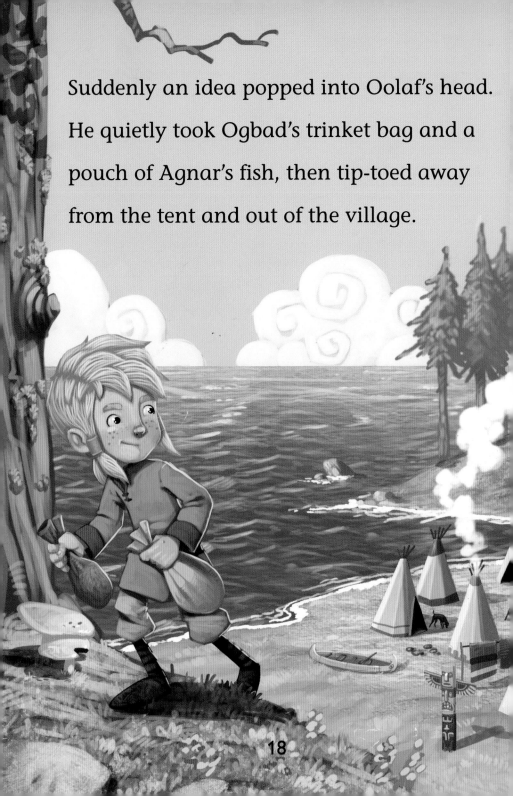

In the distance he spotted a great cloud of
dust that was getting closer. A deafening
sound filled the air and Oolaf saw that the
cloud was a herd of huge, shaggy Bison
thundering toward him ...

He squeezed his eyes shut, not daring to
look, when suddenly he felt himself lifted
onto the back of one of the beasts. The Chief
of the Plains sat in front of him, steering it
along. "Come with me!" he commanded.

The Chief listened as Oolaf told him all about the cows back home, and about the voyage. Then Oolaf gave him some Viking trinkets, and some of Agnar's fish! "We will make you a new sail from Buffalo skin," gasped the Chief, rubbing the taste from his tongue.

"Great!" cried Oolaf. Then he explained that he had somewhere he must go, but would be back later. Off he ran.

Chapter Four

Soon he came to a great lake that shone like a mirror. "It's nearly as big as the sea!" he gasped. He went right to the muddy edge for a better look, but it was awfully slippery and Oolaf went tumbling into the water.

"Help!" he spluttered as he felt something pulling at his clothes. A huge snapping turtle was dragging him to the bottom!

Suddenly he felt himself dragged back up again by The Chief of the Great Lakes. "Come with me," he boomed.

The Chief listened in amazement as Oolaf told him all about the icy lakes back home, and all about the voyage. Then Oolaf gave him the last handful of Viking trinkets, and a taste of Agnar's pickled fish ...

"We will weave you some rope," the Chief said, spitting out the fish. "Great!" cried Oolaf. "When you've finished there's someone I want you to meet."

23

Chapter Five

The Vikings and Tuk still hadn't noticed that Oolaf had disappeared, when they heard a commotion outside the tent. Standing there were The Chief of the Plains, The Chief of the Great Lakes, and a very pleased-looking Oolaf with a brand new sail and lots of rope.

The three Chiefs spoke and all agreed that they should work together to help the Vikings get back home.

"Not far from here is a forest full of tall trees to make the planks for your boat," Tuk said.

"But a tribe of Giants – the Genoskwa – live there, and they'll surely gobble you up!"

They took the Vikings to the edge of the
forest, but were too scared to follow them.
Harald spotted the perfect tree and Erik
swung his axe. CHOP! CHOP! CHOP!

A ghastly howl filled the air. Crashing through the trees came the biggest, hairiest creatures the Vikings had ever seen!

The creatures began uprooting trees and hurling them through the air. They crashed down around the Vikings, trapping them.

WHIZZ, WHIZZ, WHIZZ! The three Chiefs were firing arrows into the forest, and skewered onto each one was one of Agnar's pickled fish. The Giants found the fish so delicious that they forgot about the Vikings.

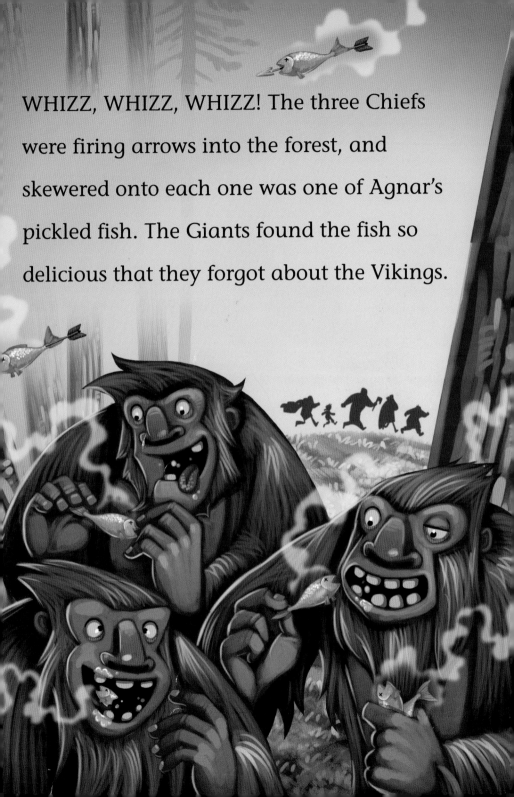

A few days later, the Vikings had built a beautiful new boat. They thanked the Chiefs for their help and promised to come back one day. "I think I'll call this place *Pink Point*," said Harald.

"No – *Stormy Point!*" said Oolaf.

Harald Forkbeard stood on the beach, watching a flock of squawking birds fly past. "Where next, son?" he asked Oolaf.

Oolaf scratched his chin and pointed to the horizon. "Home!" he replied.

Viking facts in the story

Genoskwa The name given by the Native American group of people known as the Iroquois to a hairy race of giants who lived in the forests. The Viking explorer Leif Erikson claimed to have encountered such hairy giants, in the New World in 986 CE.

Sun Stone Thought to be a magical gem in the Icelandic sagas. Most likely to be a piece of Feldspar (group of minerals) which radiated the sun's rays even on cloudy days. Because the Vikings didn't use maps, they relied on nature to get around.

Sea Serpent The Vikings believed these lived beneath the sea, and coiled around the world.

Pink Point/ Stormy Point The Vikings had a settlement in Newfoundland at *L'Anse aux Meadows* but evidence of one was found 600 km further South, at a place called *Stormy Point*, now known as *Point Rosee* or *Pink Point*.